The Littles
Make a Friend

The Littles
Make a Friend

Adapted by **Teddy Slater**
from **THE LITTLES**
by **John Peterson**
Illustrated by **Jacqueline Rogers**

SCHOLASTIC INC.
New York Toronto London Auckland Sydney
Mexico City New Delhi Hong Kong

Mr. and Mrs. Little were
barely six inches small.
Their children, Tom and
Lucy, were even shorter.
So was Granny Little.

All the Littles had nice long tails.
Except for that, they looked just
like you and me.

The whole family lived in
the walls of Mr. and Mrs.
Bigg's house.
They got all they needed
from the Biggs.

A yummy Bigg dinner scrap made
a fine meal for a hungry Little.
A torn sock was a cozy Little
sleeping bag.

The Biggs had no idea
the Littles were there.
But the Littles could
see and hear the Biggs
quite easily.

One day they heard the Biggs

planning their summer vacation.

Another family was going

to stay in the house while they

were gone.

"I hope they don't have

a cat," Lucy said.

The other Littles nodded.

They were all afraid of cats.

The Littles felt better when
the new people moved in.
Mr. and Mrs. Newcomb
did not have a cat. There
was only one problem....

The Newcombs turned out
to be terrible housekeepers.
Before long, the house
was a total mess.

Granny wagged her finger.

"Mark my words," she said.

"There will soon be mice

in this house."

And so there were.

The Newcombs did not

even notice.

But the Littles sure did.

A mouse to a Little is as scary as

a lion is to you and me.

"We have to make the
Newcombs see the horrid
beasts," said Mr. Little.
"Then they will set traps."

15

The Littles had a family meeting.

"I have an idea," said Tom.

"I could dress up like a mouse

and run right under Mrs.

Newcomb's nose.

I bet she'd notice that."

Tom's plan sounded dangerous,
but no one had a better idea.
Granny Little picked up her
needle and thread and went
to work.

The mouse suit was a perfect fit!

Granny had made ears and whiskers.

But, of course, she didn't need

to make a tail.

There was no time to lose.

Tom dashed into the

kitchen, right between

Mrs. Newcomb's feet.

"EEEEK!" Mrs. Newcomb screamed.

"A mouse!"

The Littles jumped up and down.

They were sure Tom's plan had

worked.

But no, the Newcombs didn't get

a mousetrap....

They got a cat instead —

a big, hairy, scary cat!

"Oh, no!" Lucy said.
"One cat is worse than
a million mice. It will
eat us all."

"Not if we can tame it,"
Tom said.

"Cats have always been
friends to big people —
why not to us?"

Granny wasn't sure.

"A cat is no friend to

a Little," she said.

But Mr. Little said,

"It's worth a try."

They found the cat in
the cellar.
Mr. Little rolled a ball
of yarn toward her.
He had heard that cats
like yarn.

The cat woke up.

She looked at the yarn.

She looked at the Littles.

Uh-oh.

"Here, kitty, kitty,"
Tom said bravely.
The cat cocked her
head at the sound
of his voice.

Suddenly the cat made

a soft, humming sound.

Tom reached up and

touched her fur.

"Nice kitty," he said.

The humming got louder.

"I think she's purring,"

Tom said.

"That means she likes us."

"It must have been the
talking," said Mr. Little.
"I don't think she knew
we were people until
she heard Tom speak."

From then on, Tom
and the cat were friends.
The two friends went
everywhere together.
And all the mice went
somewhere else!